Jack
and the
LeanStalk

a fractured fairytale by
Raven Howell
illustrated by
Sarah Gledhill

atmosphere press

For Talis, may a fairytale never stray far from your heart.

Jack and his parents, Mr. and Mrs. Garbanzo,
live on their farm in the town of Pinto.

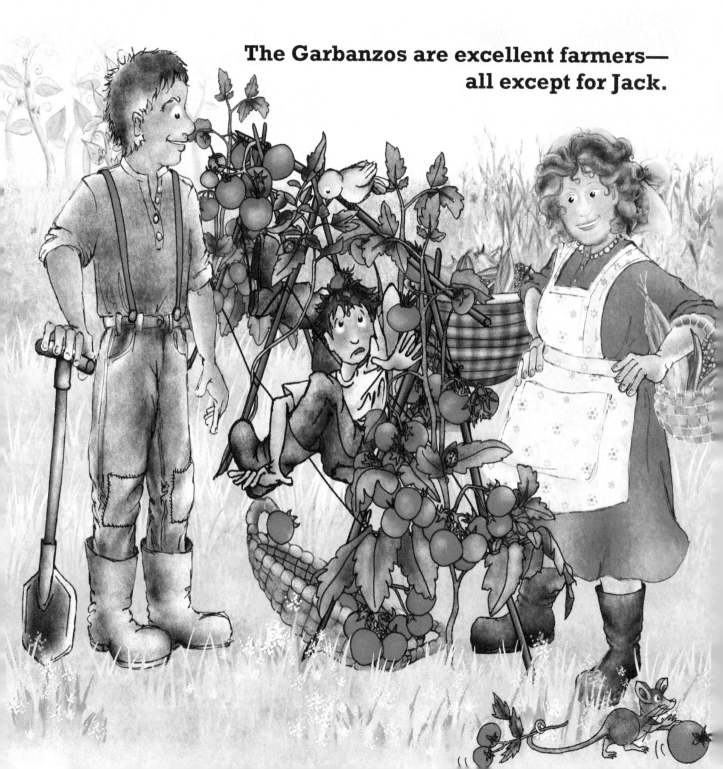

The Garbanzos are excellent farmers— all except for Jack.

Instead, Jack's the one townspeople approach to mend fences and repair sheds. He built the bookshelves for Pinto's library and the beautiful oak porch at the town inn – a cozy place that many like to visit.

The past year, while the farm's corn and tomatoes filled baskets, there were no beans.

Dark clouds appeared to hover over the bean field. Once there had been rows and rows of mile-long magical beanstalks stretching up into the sunny sky as far as the eye could see, but now the stalks had turned thin, losing their enchantment.

Earlier in the season, a Giant appeared.

The Giant had green skin and droopy eyes. Wildflowers seemed to sprout from his big ears. Peering out from the Giant's overall pocket, a grumpy frog would stick out his tongue, grumbling a croak.

The community did not like the clumsy Giant child who didn't look like them.

"You've no place here in Pinto," the townspeople called out.

"You stink!" and "You're ugly!" exclaimed the school children, rudely pointing and then running away.

His feelings hurt, the Giant hid away in the Garbanzo bean field. Every evening the neighbors would hear his moans and cries, and the ground would tremble. The soil in the field became soggy. The beans disappeared, leaving only a few lean stalks. Not one townsperson was brave enough or kind enough to approach the miserable Giant.

One morning while the Garbanzos were breakfasting, plates full of eggs and wild blueberry pancakes, Jack's father cleared his throat and unhappily announced, "I'm afraid our farm can't be maintained without the bean crop."

Jack stopped eating mid-bite and looked up, surprised. He wanted to help, but his farming skills were terrible. Jack couldn't even get a carrot seed to sprout, let alone get dandelions to multiply (and we all know how dandelions like doing so), but he felt something had to be done.

A daring idea came to him. Jack knew it was going to take courage. He took a deep breath, smiled weakly at his father, and poured more maple syrup on his pancakes.

That evening Jack slipped out of bed. He dressed quickly, pulling on his favorite hooded sweatshirt. Tiptoeing outdoors, he straightened his shoulders and followed the moonlit path toward the bean field.

As he approached the Giant slowly and cautiously, the Giant sniffed the air and called out, "If you care, harrumph, harrumph, you'll stop right there, harrumph, harrumph!"

Jack paused just as his sneaker crunched down loudly on a twig underfoot, breaking it in two.

Before he could lose his courage, he stuttered, "Giant, why do you cry?"

Cheeks wet, the Giant turned to him.

"The townspeople bully me. I know I look different, but no one has given me a chance. I'm a nice guy . . . well, Giant. I miss my mom, dad, and my cat, Puss 'N Boots."

Jack sighed, looking up at the Giant, "That is sad, but your giant tears flood our field. Why don't you go home?"

The Giant continued in a trembling voice. "I can't get back. My home, in the land of Cloud, is at the top of the highest beanstalks. I've tried climbing up many times, but the beanstalks are lean and no longer enchanted. I end up swaying back and forth and toppling down!"

That explained the earth shakes!

"Getting here was not a problem. I slipped down so easily from Cloud. The beanstalks were strong and healthy, but I'm much too giant to scramble back up the weak vines now," the Giant said gloomily.

With that, he exploded in another burst of grief and despair. Jack patiently waited while the Giant took a handkerchief from the frog in his pocket and blew his big nose.

"Giant," said Jack gently. "Your tears drown the bean plants. They are struggling to grow."

Shaken, the Giant drew in a quick breath and responded, "I'm so sorry. I love beans! They're my very favorite snack. I came to this field because they give me some comfort. That, and I miss my mom's cooking!"

In the Giant's sadness, he'd been eating beans, crying, and flooding the field. His tears were the very reason he couldn't go home. A tragedy if Jack ever heard of one! Poor Giant.

The two companions sat down under the oak tree and quietly contemplated the dilemma.

The Giant wasn't ugly. He didn't "stink" like some of his schoolmates had suggested. In fact, when the Giant put his gigantic chummy arm around Jack's shoulders, Jack didn't mind at all, knowing he'd made a friend.

"I've got it!" exclaimed Jack. His face flushed and voice rose as he began to explain his plan. The Giant's eyes grew wide as he gave a loud guffaw. Then delighted, he clapped his hands together with a missing tooth grin.

The next morning's sun rose warm and bright. Jack jumped from bed and rushed down to meet his parents at the kitchen table.

Before anyone could take a bite of Mrs. Garbanzo's hot buttered biscuits, Jack excitedly told Mr. and Mrs. Garbanzo of the previous night's adventures.

"Jack, it's dangerous sneaking out at night," said Mrs. Garbanzo.

"And to meet with the Giant!" added his father.

Still, they had to admit it was brave and kind-hearted to reach out to this lonely, bullied Giant.

Jack pleaded, "No one has given the Giant an opportunity – he's not that different from the rest of us. He feels lost and misses his family! I may not be helpful at farming, but I am good at woodworking. I want to help our Giant friend by building him a grand staircase along the tallest beanstalk left. It would be a passage back home to Cloud."

Mr. Garbanzo was proud of Jack. He perked up. "It sounds promising! You're giving the Giant hope, and it may save our bean crop and farm. If anyone can do this – it's you!"

Mrs. Garbanzo's eyes twinkled and she smiled, passing Jack the strawberry jam.

In the following weeks Jack worked hard from sunrise to sunset.

While the staircase was developing into a beautiful and graceful path to the skyline, the Giant was invited into the Garbanzo household. The Three Bears checked, but even they did not have a bed large enough for the Giant to sleep in. Instead, Mr. Garbanzo set up a tent in the middle of Jack's bedroom.

Jack and the Giant spent evenings laughing, sharing stories and creating shadow trolls on the tent walls with flashlights. Mrs. Garbanzo made sure they both had plenty of her delicious black bean dip and chips to munch on.

By summer's end, the bean fields started growing back, more magical than before.

Townspeople changed their minds about the Giant.

Even the children came to watch Jack build his staircase and play ball with the Giant. He untangled kite strings from treetops and gave them gleeful piggyback rides. That made the frog in the Giant's pocket quite cranky, but that's another story about frogs and their wish to be kissed by princesses.

Before the first day of school began, Jack's spiral staircase successfully encircled the tallest beanstalk. When the final step was built, Jack and the Giant said goodbye, promising to remain friends. Their journey was coming to an end.

Many hugs were exchanged. Everyone watched and waved as the Giant joyfully climbed Jack's staircase to his home.

The End

About Atmosphere Press

Atmosphere Press is an independent, full-service publisher for excellent books in all genres and for all audiences. Learn more about what we do at atmospherepress.com.

We encourage you to check out some of Atmosphere's latest children's releases, which are available at Amazon.com and via order from your local bookstore:

Young Yogi and the Mind Monsters, by Sonja Radvila

Buried Treasure, a picture book by Anne Krebbs

The Magpie and The Turtle, a Native American-inspired folk tale by Timothy Yeahquo, Jr.

The Alligator Wrestler: A Girls Can Do Anything Book, by Carmen Petro

My WILD First Day of School, a picture book by Dennis Mathew

I Will Love You Forever and Always, a picture book by Sarah M. Thomas Mariano

The Sky Belongs to the Dreamers, a picture book by J.P. Hostetler

Shooting Stars, A Girls Can Do Anything Book, by Carmen Petro

Carpenters and Catapults, A Girls Can Do Anything Book, by Carmen Petro

Gone Fishing, A Girls Can Do Anything Book, by Carmen Petro

Owlfred the Owl Learns to Fly, a picture book by Caleb Foster

Bello the Cello, a picture book by Dennis Mathew

That Scarlett Bacon, a picture book by Mark Johnson

About the Author

Raven Howell is an award-winning children's picture book author and poet. She writes poetry for a variety of children's magazines including *Highlights*, *Humpty Dumpty*, *Cricket*, and *The School Magazine*. Sharing book events and advocating writing and poetry with students in schools and libraries, Raven also serves as Creative & Publishing Advisor with RedClover Reader. She resides and writes in the mountainous Hudson Valley.

Influenced by the delightfully whimsical literary world of fairy and folk tales from childhood, Raven's *Jack and the Lean Stalk* blends old-fashioned themes to modern day relevance.

About the Illustrator

Sarah Gledhill lives in Yorkshire, United Kingdom. Having spent decades bouncing around the hot African veld in a Landi, sharing life and adventures with four sons and a wonderful variety of animals, she is now happily rediscovering the cherished and increasingly fragile worlds of the inhabitants of the hedgerows, woodlands, and dry stone walls of the UK.

CPSIA information can be obtained
at www.ICGtesting.com
Printed in the USA
BVHW012053190520
579979BV00003B/155